The Front Hall Carpet

by Nicholas Heller

GREENWILLOW BOOKS, New York

For the Conte family

Watercolor and acrylic paints and a
black pen were used for the full-color art.
The text type is Brighton Light.

Printed in Singapore by Tien Wah Press
First Edition

10 9 8 7 6 5 4 3 2 1

Library of Congress
Cataloging-in-Publication Data

Heller, Nicholas.
The front hall carpet / Nicholas Heller.
p. cm.
Summary: A youngster lives in a house
where a blue river flows in the front hall,
a grassy green field covers the dining room,
and a maze traps night monsters in the bedroom.
ISBN 0-688-05272-X.
ISBN 0-688-05273-8 (lib. bdg.)
[1. Rugs—Fiction.] I. Title.
PZ7.H37426Fr 1990
[E]—dc20 89-38360 CIP AC

Our front hall carpet is blue like a river.

Sometimes I go on canoe trips

and catch speckled trout for lunch.

And sometimes I go swimming with the crocodiles.

The dining room carpet is as green as a grassy field.

It's perfect for a game of croquet

or a picnic and a nap in the shade of a cherry tree.

The tile floor in the kitchen is like a jewel-studded palace.

A long hallway leads to the throne room

where I sit and rule my loyal subjects.

There's a white, shaggy bear in our living room.

He's my friend and lets me ride on his back through the snow.

Often we see seals, and penguins floating by on icebergs.

When it gets too cold, we stop and drink hot tea with an Eskimo.

My parents have a polka-dot rug in their bedroom.

When I'm wearing red, I can only step on the red dots.

And when I'm wearing green, I have to step on the green ones.

But when I have my polka-dot pajamas on, I can step wherever I like.

My favorite carpet is the one in my room. It's a maze.

Only I know how it works.

If any monsters try to follow me at night, they're sure to get lost.

But if you're coming to say good night,
then perhaps I'll show you the way through.